AF427169

ANONYMOUS

Life Goes On

a play

Copyright © 2024 by anonymous

All rights reserved. No part of this publication may be reproduced, stored or transmitted in any form or by any means, electronic, mechanical, photocopying, recording, scanning, or otherwise without written permission from the publisher. It is illegal to copy this book, post it to a website, or distribute it by any other means without permission.

This novel is entirely a work of fiction. The names, characters and incidents portrayed in it are the work of the author's imagination. Any resemblance to actual persons, living or dead, events or localities is entirely coincidental.

anonymous is NOT trying to promote suicide.

First edition

This book was professionally typeset on Reedsy.
Find out more at reedsy.com

To my mother...
for teaching me that life,
no matter how heavy,
goes on.

Contents

Foreword

This play is a reflection on the impermanence of life and the enduring passage of time, themes that often linger at the edges of our consciousness but rarely find their way into the open. It doesn't seek to provide answers or comfort; rather, it invites the audience to confront the uncomfortable reality that, in the end, life moves forward with or without us.

"Life Goes On" is not a story of tragedy alone, but one of everyday existence continuing beyond loss. It depicts the unspoken truth that grief, while profound, is fleeting in the grander scheme of life's relentless progression. It shows us how memories can fade, even of those we thought unforgettable, and how even the most devastating moments can dissolve into the background of new routines and experiences.

This play does not focus on the reasons behind Bianca's choice or delve into her inner turmoil. Instead, it brings to light the aftermath—the unsettling normalcy that follows such an irrevocable act. It is about those left behind: the friends who find laughter again, the parents who return to their routines, and the spaces that, once emptied, are filled by others. It challenges the often-romanticized notion of leaving a lasting impact and instead presents a stark truth: the world moves on.

"Life Goes On" does not offer solace or closure. It is a mirror held up to the reality of loss, a reminder that even when we feel like the world should stop, it never does. In its silence and stillness, it asks us to reflect on our own lives and the lives of those around us, and to consider what it means to be remembered—or to be forgotten.

This play is not just a story—it is an experience. One that is meant to leave a lingering echo long after the curtain falls. An echo that, much like life itself, fades with time but never quite disappears.

Acknowledgments

Special thanks to KoolShooters from Pexels for the powerful photograph featured on the cover. Your work beautifully captures the mood and essence of this play, adding depth and visual emotion to the story told within these pages.

Characters

Bianca: A high school student who seems well-adjusted and happy on the surface. She is sociable, kind, and blends seamlessly into her group of friends and school environment. Her reasons for choosing suicide remain unknown, leaving her inner world a mystery.

Mother: Bianca's mother. Portrayed as loving but emotionally distant. She is caught in the routines of everyday life, and her grief, while initially overwhelming, gradually fades as she settles back into these routines.

Father: Bianca's father. Like her mother, he is caring but somewhat detached. His grief manifests through quiet moments and is later overshadowed by the return to mundane daily tasks and responsibilities.

Friend 1: One of Bianca's friends, seen interacting with her in lighter moments at school and later moving on with new friendships and activities. Represents the ordinary teenager who is swept along with life's flow, only momentarily touched by Bianca's absence.

Friend 2: Another of Bianca's friends. Engages in conversations and activities that show how life resumes its course after

Bianca's death. Embodies the fleeting nature of grief in the broader social circle.

Friend 3: Part of Bianca's friend group, appearing in scenes that depict both the normalcy of their high school life and their eventual moving on. Reflects the theme of emotional distance that develops over time.

New Student: A student who takes over Bianca's seat in the classroom. Represents the continuity of life and the replacement of what is lost, even if unknowingly.

Priest/Officiant: The figure who conducts Bianca's funeral service. Their presence highlights the ritual of mourning and the universal experiences of loss and burial.

Teacher: A high school teacher who remains focused on the daily routine of education. Appears in scenes depicting the classroom, emphasizing how life continues unabated in structured environments like schools.

Various Students: Background characters who populate the school environment, the café, and other public spaces. They reflect the collective movement of life, indifferent to individual loss.

Mourners: Present at the funeral, representing the mix of family, friends, and community members who mourn, but also quickly return to their own lives.

Crow: A symbolic presence at Bianca's grave. Its appearance adds to the stark imagery of abandonment and the passage of time.

Jogger, Couple, Child with Parent: Minor characters who populate the park scenes and symbolize the ongoing, unaffected rhythms of life amidst personal loss.

Background Extras: Various unnamed characters who appear throughout the play in different settings—school, café, homes, park, and cemetery—to create a sense of a world that continues beyond Bianca's story.

I

Act 1: Normalcy

Scene 1: High School Hallway

[The stage is set to resemble a typical high school hallway in 2011. There are rows of lockers lining the walls, with a few bulletin boards displaying school announcements and posters for upcoming events. The sound of indistinct chatter and the occasional slamming of lockers creates a lively atmosphere. Students mill about, some in groups, others hurrying to their next class. The lighting is bright and warm, evoking the everyday energy of a school day.]

[Bianca enters from stage left, holding a textbook in one hand and a phone in the other. She is dressed casually, her style fitting in with the fashion of 2011—jeans, a simple top, and a light jacket. She walks with a relaxed confidence, smiling as she navigates the crowd.]

Friend 1
(approaching Bianca with a grin)
Bianca! Did you finish the history homework? I was up all night with that thing.

Bianca
(laughing as she tucks her phone into her pocket)

Of course I did. I had to, otherwise, Mr. Harris would have a field day. He loves catching us off guard.

Friend 2

(joining the conversation, holding a water bottle)
You're a lifesaver, seriously. Can I borrow your notes later? I was so zoned out in class.

Bianca

(playfully rolling her eyes)
Sure, but you owe me one. Maybe you can cover me in gym class today?

Friend 2

Deal! You know I've got your back. *(glancing at the time on their phone)* Hey, we should get to English before the bell rings. Ms. Thompson's been on a warpath lately.

[As they walk down the hallway together, Bianca glances at a poster on the bulletin board advertising the upcoming school dance. She nudges Friend 1 and points at the poster.]

Bianca

Are you going to the dance? I heard it's supposed to be amazing this year.

Friend 1

(shrugging with a smile)
Maybe. Depends on if someone asks me. What about you? Any secret admirers?

Bianca

(*teasing*)

Wouldn't you like to know? But seriously, I might just go with a group. No pressure, just fun.

[They stop at Bianca's locker, which she opens with a practiced twist of the combination lock. Inside, the locker is neat, with a few personal items—a photo of her and her friends, some textbooks, and a small mirror. She swaps out her books, still engaged in the conversation.]

Friend 2

Sounds like a plan. We'll all just go together, keep it simple. Who needs the drama, right?

Bianca

Exactly. It'll be fun, I promise. No awkward slow dances, just us having a good time.

[As Bianca closes her locker, another student (Friend 3) approaches, looking a bit frazzled.]

Friend 3

(*panting slightly as they rush up*)

Hey, Bianca! Do you have an extra pen? Mine just died, and I've got a test next period.

Bianca

(*smiling as she digs into her bag*)

You're in luck. Here, take this one. Just don't forget to give it back. It's my favorite.

Friend 3
(gratefully taking the pen)
You're a lifesaver! Seriously, what would I do without you?

Bianca
You'd survive somehow. But hey, don't stress about the test. You've got this.

[The school bell rings, signaling the start of the next period. The hallway begins to empty as students head to their classes. Bianca and her friends exchange quick goodbyes and head off in different directions.]

Bianca
(waving as she starts to walk offstage)
See you guys at lunch!

Friends
(in unison)

Later, Bianca!

[Bianca walks offstage, her smile lingering as she disappears from view. The stage gradually empties, leaving behind the quiet echoes of the bustling hallway. The lights dim slightly, signaling the end of the scene.]

[End Scene 1]

Scene 2: Bianca's Home

[The stage is set to resemble a modest, cozy family home with a combined living room and dining area. The living room has a comfortable sofa, a coffee table with a few magazines, and a television turned off in the corner. The dining area is adjacent, featuring a small wooden table with three chairs. The lighting is warm, creating an inviting atmosphere that feels typical and familiar.]

[Bianca enters from stage left, carrying a backpack. She drops it near the living room sofa and heads toward the dining table where her mother is already seated. The mother is setting down a simple meal—plates of pasta, a salad bowl, and a jug of water. The father enters from the right, holding a newspaper and wearing reading glasses. He takes his seat without much fanfare.]

Mother
(cheerfully, as she places a bowl of salad in the center of the table)
Dinner's ready! Bianca, wash your hands, please.

Bianca
(nodding as she heads off to a sink in the corner and washes her

hands)
Sure thing, Mom. Smells great.

Father
(folding his newspaper neatly and setting it aside)
Had a busy day, kiddo? You seemed to rush in pretty quick.

Bianca
(drying her hands on a towel and moving to take a seat at the table)
Yeah, it was okay. Just the usual stuff—school, homework, trying to stay awake in Mr. Harris's class.

Mother
(chuckling as she serves the pasta)
That bad, huh? Maybe he'll retire soon, and you'll get someone more exciting.

Bianca
(laughs lightly)
One can only hope.

[They all begin to eat. The atmosphere is calm and relaxed, but there's a noticeable routine to their actions. The clinking of cutlery and plates fills the silence between their words.]

Father
(taking a sip of water, looking at Bianca)
Any plans for the weekend? I think your cousin has a birthday coming up. We might drop by for a bit.

Bianca
(*nods while chewing, then swallows*)
Yeah, I was thinking of going to the dance on Friday. Maybe stay over at a friend's afterward.

Mother
(*mildly interested*)
That sounds nice. You've been working hard lately; a little fun wouldn't hurt.

Father
(*half-heartedly, while still focused on his food*)
Just make sure you're home at a decent hour, or let us know if you're staying over. Don't want to wake up to an empty house.

Bianca
(*smiling, nodding along*)
Got it, Dad. I'll keep you posted.

[There's a brief silence as they continue eating. The father glances at the newspaper beside him, still partially in his thoughts, while the mother refills her glass of water.]

Mother
(*casually, as if filling a void in the conversation*)
Did you hear about the new grocery store opening up downtown? They say it's got some great deals on produce.

Father
(*raising an eyebrow, sounding mildly interested*)
Really? We should check it out this weekend. Might save a

few bucks.

Bianca
(smirking slightly)
Thrilling stuff, you guys. Grocery stores and birthday parties—what more could we ask for?

Mother
(laughing softly, reaching out to pat Bianca's hand affectionately)
Hey, when you're our age, that's exciting.

[They all share a small, knowing smile. The moment is comfortable, but there's a sense that they're simply going through the motions.]

Father
(leaning back slightly in his chair, glancing at Bianca)
So, any big projects coming up at school? Anything we should be worried about?

Bianca
(shaking her head, taking another bite)
Nah, just the usual tests and papers. Nothing too crazy. I've got it under control.

Mother
(nodding approvingly)
Good to hear. Just remember to balance things, okay? School's important, but so is taking care of yourself.

Bianca

(nods, her expression neutral)
Yeah, I know. I'm fine, Mom. Really.

[The conversation continues to wane, with pauses becoming more frequent. The parents focus on finishing their meal, occasionally making small talk about unremarkable daily events.]

Mother
(standing up with her plate)
Well, I think I'll make some tea. Anyone want some?

Father
(glancing at his watch, shaking his head)
Not for me. Got to catch the news in a bit.

Bianca
(standing up as well, picking up her plate)
I'm good, thanks. I've got some homework to finish anyway.

[Bianca starts to clear the table with her mother. The father picks up his newspaper again, leaning back in his chair, seemingly preparing to settle in for the evening.]

Mother
(smiling at Bianca, gently nudging her with an elbow)
Alright, don't stay up too late, okay?

Bianca
(smiling back, though her eyes seem a bit distant)
I won't. Promise.

[The scene fades out as Bianca carries the dishes to the sink. Her parents continue with their routine, each in their own world, sharing the same space but somewhat disconnected. The warm lighting gradually dims, signaling the end of the scene.]

[End Scene 2]

Scene 3: School Day

[The stage is set to represent various locations within a high school: a classroom with desks and chairs, a cafeteria area with tables, and an outdoor space with a blanket under a shady tree. The lighting changes subtly to transition between different settings, indicating the passage of time throughout a typical school day.]

[The scene opens with the classroom setting. Students are seated at their desks, and a teacher's desk is positioned at the front with a whiteboard behind it. The teacher, an older figure with glasses and a slightly disheveled appearance, is writing something on the board. The room is filled with the quiet hum of students flipping through textbooks and whispering to each other.]

Teacher
(turning to face the class, pointing to a diagram on the board)
Alright, who can explain what we discussed yesterday about photosynthesis? Bianca? Care to enlighten us?

[Bianca is seated near the middle, surrounded by other students. She looks up, a slight smile on her face, as she

closes her notebook.]

Bianca
(*confidently, yet casually*)
Sure, it's the process by which plants use sunlight to convert carbon dioxide and water into glucose and oxygen. Basically, it's how they make their food.

Teacher
(*nodding approvingly*)
Exactly. And why is this process vital for life on Earth?

Bianca
(*after a brief pause, thinking aloud*)
Because it's the foundation of the food chain, and it also produces oxygen, which we need to breathe.

Teacher
(*smiling, pleased with the answer*)
Right on the mark, as always. Thanks, Bianca.

[The bell rings, signaling the end of the class. Students start packing their bags and heading out. The lights dim slightly, shifting to the next setting: the cafeteria.]

[The cafeteria setting features a few tables scattered around. There's the typical noise of a school lunch period—students talking, laughing, and the faint clatter of trays and cutlery. Bianca is sitting with two friends at a table near the center. They're eating lunch, laughing, and enjoying their break.]

Friend 1

(mid-bite, looking amused)

So, wait—you're telling me you really convinced him it was "National Skip Gym Day"? How did he believe that?

Bianca

(grinning, taking a sip of her drink)

He's new! Plus, I was very convincing. I even showed him a fake flyer I printed out. Poor guy's probably hiding out in the library right now.

Friend 2

(laughing, nearly spilling their drink)

You're terrible! But honestly, I would've believed you too. Anything to get out of running laps.

Bianca

(laughs along, shrugging innocently)

Hey, I'm just trying to make life a little more interesting.

[The conversation continues, filled with light banter and laughter. The atmosphere is relaxed and carefree, with no hint of anything out of the ordinary. The lights transition to the next setting: the outdoor area.]

[The outdoor area is set under a shady tree with a large blanket spread out on the grass. Bianca and her friends are lounging on the blanket, some sitting up, others lying down. The scene has a calm, serene feel with a gentle breeze rustling through the leaves. A few students are playing Frisbee or chatting in the background.]

Friend 3

(lying back, staring up at the sky)
I swear, if I could stay out here all day, I'd never set foot in a classroom again.

Bianca

(sitting cross-legged, picking at the grass absentmindedly)
Who says we can't? Let's start a petition—'More Time Under Trees Initiative.' I'll be the president.

Friend 1

(laughs, sitting up and tossing a small pebble at Bianca)
You and your grand plans, always trying to change the world.

Bianca

(mock serious, pretending to hold a microphone)
Well, someone's got to do it. And if it means more naps under this tree, I'm all in.

Friend 2

(smiling, flipping through a magazine)
Seriously though, this is the best part of the day. Just hanging out and doing nothing. No tests, no teachers, just us.

[The friends continue to chat and joke, sharing small anecdotes about their day. The mood remains light and carefree, a typical moment of teenage relaxation. The lights shift subtly again, moving to the next location: an extracurricular club meeting room.]

[The new setting shows a small room with a few chairs

arranged in a semi-circle. There's a large whiteboard with notes and doodles, indicating it's a club meeting of some sort. Bianca sits among a small group of students, listening attentively as another student speaks at the front.]

Student Leader
(animated, holding up a clipboard)
Okay, so for the next project, we're going to need volunteers to help with set design. It's going to be a bit of work, but I promise, it'll be fun. Bianca, are you in?

Bianca
(nods enthusiastically, raising her hand)
Yeah, count me in. I love painting, so I'm happy to help with the backdrops.

Student Leader
(smiling, jotting it down)
Great! We'll meet after school tomorrow to get started. Thanks, Bianca!

[The meeting continues with more planning and discussion. Bianca is engaged, contributing ideas and participating actively. The atmosphere is collaborative and positive. The lights dim as the meeting comes to a close, transitioning back to the outdoor area for a final, brief moment.]

[Back at the outdoor area, the sun is beginning to set, casting a warm, golden glow. Bianca and her friends are still on the blanket, laughing about a joke someone just

told. The scene is peaceful, and the day is winding down.]

Friend 3
(sitting up, stretching)
Alright, I guess we should head home. It's getting late.

Bianca
(nods, starting to gather her things)
Yeah, I've got a mountain of homework waiting for me. Fun times.

Friend 1
(smiling, giving Bianca a playful nudge)
You know you love it. The future valedictorian never sleeps!

Bianca
(laughing, slinging her bag over her shoulder)
Maybe. But even valedictorians need their beauty sleep. See you guys tomorrow!

Friends
(in unison, waving)
Later, Bianca!

[The friends disperse, heading offstage in different directions. Bianca lingers for a moment, looking around with a faint smile, before exiting. The lights slowly fade, signaling the end of the scene.]

[End Scene 3]

II

Act 2: Commit

Scene 1: Bianca's Room

[The stage is set to resemble a teenage girl's bedroom. The room is modestly decorated with a bed against one wall, a small desk cluttered with schoolbooks and a few personal items, and a wardrobe near the corner. Posters and photographs are pinned to the walls—pictures of friends, scenic places, and a few inspirational quotes. The lighting is dim, casting soft shadows that create an intimate and slightly somber atmosphere. There is a single window that allows a sliver of light to filter in, suggesting the fading hours of the day.]

[Bianca enters the room slowly, closing the door behind her with a soft click. She stands still for a moment, her back against the door, her eyes scanning the room. The space feels quiet, almost heavy, with a sense of stillness settling over it. Her movements are slow and deliberate, contrasting sharply with the liveliness seen in previous scenes.]

[She walks over to her desk and places her hand on an open notebook, lightly running her fingers over the pages filled with her handwriting. She lingers for a moment, her expression unreadable, before closing the notebook gently and pushing it aside. She then opens a drawer and takes out a small object—a bottle of pills. She holds it in her hand, staring at it intently, her face still and contemplative.]

[Bianca turns and moves towards her bed. She sits down on the edge, still holding the bottle, her gaze distant. She remains there for a few seconds, her shoulders slightly hunched as if weighed down by an invisible burden. She places the bottle on the bed beside her, and then reaches for a glass of water on her nightstand. She holds the glass, her grip tightening for a moment, before setting it back down. Her breaths are steady but deep, as if she is bracing herself.]

[The room is enveloped in a quiet stillness, broken only by the faint sounds of the world outside—a distant car passing by, the rustle of leaves against the window. The light through the window grows dimmer, casting long shadows across the room, creating a sense of isolation and introspection.]

[Bianca stands up slowly, moving with purpose but without haste. She walks over to the wardrobe and opens it, pulling out a hoodie and slipping it on. She glances at herself briefly in a small mirror hanging on the inside of the wardrobe door. Her expression remains calm, almost resigned. She closes the wardrobe door quietly and takes a deep breath as if grounding herself in the moment.]

[She moves back to the bed and sits down again. She

picks up the bottle of pills, her movements methodical and deliberate. She opens the bottle, pouring a few pills into her hand. She pauses, looking down at them, her eyes reflecting a mix of determination and uncertainty. The pause lingers, stretching out as if time itself has slowed down.]

[After a few seconds, she puts the pills back into the bottle, her hand trembling slightly. She closes the bottle, sets it back on the bed, and leans forward, her elbows on her knees, burying her face in her hands. She stays like this for a moment, her breathing deep and measured. The room remains silent, the tension building as the audience is left to contemplate her next move.]

[Bianca slowly lifts her head and stands up, her movements now more purposeful. She walks over to the window and looks out, her face illuminated by the last traces of daylight. She closes her eyes for a moment, taking a long, deep breath. When she opens her eyes, there is a faint, almost imperceptible shift in her expression—a moment of acceptance.]

[She turns away from the window and moves back to the bed one last time. She picks up the bottle of pills again, and this time, she doesn't hesitate. She opens it, pours several pills into her hand, and brings them to her mouth. She picks up the glass of water, her hands steady, and drinks. The act is slow, deliberate, and heavy with finality. She places the glass back on the nightstand, and then sits back against the headboard, her eyes closing slowly as she swallows.]

[The lighting dims even further, the shadows growing longer, enveloping the room in an eerie calm. The faint sounds from outside fade away, leaving only the sound of Bianca's breathing, which becomes more labored. She remains still, her eyes closed, her body beginning to slump slightly as the effects of the pills start to take hold. The room darkens further, creating a sense of impending dread and uncertainty.]

[Bianca's breathing becomes shallower, her face contorting slightly with discomfort. She tries to shift her position but finds herself weak and unsteady. Her head tilts back against the wall, her eyelids fluttering. The tension builds as the room becomes almost entirely dark, save for a faint spotlight on Bianca's still figure. The scene holds for a moment longer, letting the silence and darkness settle in.]

[End Scene 1]

Scene 2: The Act

[The stage remains set as Bianca's bedroom. The lighting is dim and eerie, with shadows casting elongated, distorted shapes across the walls. The atmosphere is thick with tension and a sense of impending dread. The room is mostly silent, except for the faint hum of outside noises—a distant car, a dog barking, the wind rustling the trees.]

[Bianca is lying back against her bed, her head tilted against the headboard, her eyes half-closed. The empty pill bottle lies on the bed beside her, and the glass of water is half-empty on the nightstand. Her breathing is shallow and labored, her body already showing signs of weakness. She appears calm at first, but there is a growing tension in the room, a sense that something is about to break.]

[Suddenly, Bianca's body jerks slightly. Her face contorts in discomfort, her hand moving to her stomach as a wave of pain ripples through her. She tries to shift her position, but her movements are slow, heavy. Her breathing becomes more erratic, shallow gasps escaping her lips as the effects of the pills begin to overwhelm her system.]

[A low, guttural sound escapes her throat as her body convulses involuntarily. Her hand clutches at her abdomen, her fingers digging into her skin as if trying to hold herself together. She lets out a strained, almost inaudible groan, her face twisting in agony. Her legs twitch uncontrollably, her body writhing against the bed, struggling against the waves of pain crashing over her.]

[Her eyes open wide, panic now evident. She leans forward suddenly, her hands grasping at the bedspread, trying to find some stability. Her breath comes in ragged bursts, her chest heaving with the effort. She tries to stand, but her legs buckle beneath her, and she collapses to the floor, her body convulsing violently.]

[On the floor, she doubles over, her arms wrapped around her midsection as her body continues to spasm. She vomits suddenly and violently, the sound harsh and echoing in the quiet room. The contents spill onto the floor, mixing with her spit and the blood that begins to trickle from her nose and mouth. Her body shakes with the effort, each retch bringing more blood and bile to her lips.]

[Bianca's face is flushed and streaked with tears and blood. She gasps for breath, but her throat seems to tighten, her body rejecting the air she desperately needs. Blood starts to seep from her nose, her ears, and even the corners of her eyes. She blinks rapidly, her vision blurring as the pain intensifies. Her hands reach out, grasping at empty air, searching for something to hold onto, but finding nothing.]

[Her body jerks violently again, and she rolls onto her back, her limbs spasming uncontrollably. Her head slams against the floor with a dull thud, her mouth opening in a silent scream. Blood begins to pool beneath her, trickling from her ears and the back of her head. Her fingers claw at the floor, scraping against the wood as her body continues to convulse.]

[Bianca's breaths come in short, desperate gasps. She turns onto her side, curling into a fetal position as another wave of nausea hits. She vomits again, more violently this time, the bile and blood pouring out of her mouth and onto the floor. Her whole body shudders with the force, her eyes rolling back into her head momentarily.]

[The room begins to feel smaller, more claustrophobic, as the scene progresses. The dim lighting takes on a reddish hue, amplifying the sense of horror and the visceral reality of the moment. The sounds become more amplified—her ragged breathing, the sickening retching, the wet slap of blood hitting the floor—all blending into a haunting cacophony.]

[Her body continues to fight back, convulsing and writhing, her skin growing pale and clammy. Blood begins to seep from her gums, staining her teeth and lips a dark crimson. She lets out a low, pained moan, her body curling and twisting on the floor. Her hands grasp at her hair, pulling as if trying to root herself back to consciousness, but her strength is fading.]

[As time drags on, the spasms become less frequent but more intense, each one wracking her entire body. Her skin takes on a ghostly pallor, her veins standing out against the whiteness. Blood trickles from her eyes, leaving red streaks down her cheeks, mixing with her tears. Her mouth gapes open, blood bubbling at the corners as she tries to draw in a breath but fails.]

[Bianca's movements grow weaker, more disjointed. She tries to crawl, her hands slipping in the pool of blood and vomit that surrounds her. She manages to pull herself a few inches forward, but her body collapses again, twitching weakly. Her breaths become shallow and irregular, her chest barely rising and falling.]

[The light from the window dims further, casting the room in an almost twilight-like darkness. The scene seems to stretch, each second becoming an eternity. Bianca's body jerks sporadically, her muscles twitching involuntarily as the last traces of life struggle against the inevitable.]

[Blood continues to flow from her ears, nose, and mouth, pooling on the floor, a stark contrast against the dim lighting. Her eyes, once wide with fear, begin to lose focus. Her body stills for a moment, then convulses again with one last, desperate spasm. She coughs, a thick splatter of blood staining the floor before her. Her body then goes limp, her limbs falling heavy to her sides.]

[There is a lingering moment of stillness, broken only by the sound of Bianca's shallow, fading breaths. Her head tilts to the side, her eyes half-open but unseeing, staring blankly into the void. The blood continues to seep from her body, soaking into the floor. The room is eerily quiet now, except for the faint, uneven rhythm of her dying breaths.]

[As the minutes pass, her breathing becomes softer, more sporadic, each exhale more labored than the last. Her fingers twitch one final time, her chest gives a weak, shallow rise, and then... nothing. Her body is still. The room is filled with a deafening silence, only broken by the distant hum of life continuing outside, oblivious to the tragedy within these walls.]

[The light slowly fades out, leaving the stage in complete darkness, marking the end of the scene.]

[End Scene 2]

Scene 3: Discovery

[The stage is set to represent the interior of Bianca's home. The layout includes two distinct areas: Bianca's bedroom and a more public space, such as a hallway leading into a living room or kitchen. The bedroom remains dimly lit from the previous scene, with the same eerie, unsettling atmosphere. The rest of the home is lit more naturally, suggesting an ordinary afternoon or early evening. A clock on the wall shows the passage of time, indicating that hours have gone by since Bianca took the pills.]

[The scene opens with a focus on the hallway. The sound of a key turning in a lock is heard, followed by the front door opening. A parent (Mother or Father) enters, carrying a few grocery bags or a briefcase, and shuts the door behind them. They set their belongings down on a nearby table, letting out a tired sigh. The house is quiet, almost too quiet. They glance around, noticing the stillness but not immediately sensing anything amiss.]

[The parent calls out Bianca's name, expecting a reply. There is no answer. They pause for a moment, a slight frown forming on their face, and then call out again, louder this time. Still, no response. The parent looks around, a bit confused but not yet alarmed. They head toward the kitchen, beginning to put away groceries or sorting through mail, but their movements become slower, more distracted.]

[After a few moments, another family member (Mother or Father, depending on who entered first) arrives. They exchange a few words in hushed tones, mentioning that it's unusual for Bianca not to respond. There's a slight tension in their voices, a growing sense of unease. One of them decides to check her room, calling out her name again as they walk down the hallway. The other stays behind, preoccupied with their own tasks but clearly distracted.]

[As the first parent approaches Bianca's bedroom door, they knock softly at first, then a bit more forcefully. There is still no answer. They hesitate, their hand lingering on the doorknob, a creeping sense of dread settling in. They turn the knob slowly and push the door open.]

[The door creaks open, and the parent steps into the room. The dim lighting reveals the horrific scene—Bianca's body on the floor, surrounded by a pool of blood, vomit, and spilled pills. For a moment, there is a stunned silence. The parent's eyes widen, their face going pale as they process the sight before them. Their body freezes, as if time has stopped.]

[A beat passes, and then the parent lets out a guttural, panicked scream, dropping to their knees beside Bianca's lifeless body. Their hands tremble as they reach out, unsure whether to touch her, to shake her awake, or to pull back in fear. They touch her shoulder gently at first, but her body is cold, limp, and unresponsive. The reality of the situation begins to sink in.]

[The other parent, hearing the scream, rushes to the bedroom. They stop abruptly at the doorway, eyes widening in horror. For a moment, they are too stunned to move, their breath catching in their throat. They take in the sight—the blood, the lifeless body of their daughter, the desperate attempts of their partner to revive her. They let out a choked, agonized cry, their body buckling as they lean against the doorframe for support.]

[The parent by Bianca's side frantically tries to feel for a pulse, pressing fingers against her neck, her wrist, her chest, but finds nothing. They begin to sob uncontrollably, rocking back and forth, calling out Bianca's name over and over, begging for a response that never comes. Their voice breaks, filled with a mix of disbelief, anger, and overwhelming grief.]

[The second parent stumbles forward, their steps unsteady. They kneel down beside Bianca, their hands hovering over her, shaking uncontrollably. They touch her face, her hair, their own tears mixing with the blood on her cheeks. They look at the first parent, their eyes filled with a desperate, pleading question—"How? Why?" But no words come out.]

[The room fills with a haunting chorus of sobs and gasps.

The parents hold each other, their bodies shaking with grief as they cling to the cold, lifeless form of their daughter. The intensity of their pain is palpable, raw, and unfiltered, radiating throughout the room.]

[The scene lingers on this moment of devastation. The parents' cries echo, their voices breaking as they continue to call out Bianca's name, pleading for her to wake up, to be okay. Their hands are stained with blood, their faces twisted with anguish, unable to comprehend the finality of what they've discovered.]

[The house, once so quiet, now seems to echo with the sound of their grief. The living room light flickers, and the house itself seems to contract, as if the walls are closing in on this moment of unbearable loss. The contrast between the normalcy of the outer rooms and the horror within Bianca's bedroom is stark, almost surreal.]

[After what feels like an eternity, one of the parents reaches for a phone, their hand trembling as they dial emergency services. Their voice is barely coherent through the sobs as they try to explain what has happened. The other parent remains by Bianca's side, stroking her hair, whispering broken apologies and words of love, as if hoping somehow she might hear them, might come back to them.]

[The scene holds on this image: the parents enveloped in grief, surrounded by the stark, brutal evidence of their daughter's final moments. The sound of the phone call fades into a low hum, the words lost in the overwhelming weight of the moment. The lights slowly dim, leaving only a faint spotlight on the parents and Bianca's still body, capturing the intense, immediate aftermath of her death.]

[The light fades out completely, leaving the stage in darkness, the haunting echoes of the parents' cries lingering in the silence.]

[End Scene 3]

Scene 4: The Funeral

[The stage is set to resemble a cemetery on a somber, overcast day. A large tree stands to one side, its branches hanging low as if in mourning. The ground is uneven, with patches of grass interspersed with dirt. A freshly dug grave is at the center, surrounded by a small crowd of mourners dressed in dark clothing. A simple wooden casket rests on a platform above the open grave, draped with a few wilting flowers. The lighting is dim and muted, casting long shadows across the ground, adding to the atmosphere of grief and solemnity.]

[A priest or officiant stands at the head of the grave, holding a small book. They speak softly, but their words are indistinct—a low murmur that blends with the rustling of leaves in the wind. The crowd is gathered in a loose semicircle around the grave, heads bowed, their faces heavy with sorrow. The atmosphere is thick with the weight of unspoken emotions and the finality of the moment.]

[Bianca's parents stand closest to the casket, holding each other for support. Their faces are etched with a profound grief that goes beyond the immediate loss. The mother clutches a tissue in one hand, dabbing at her eyes and nose as silent tears stream down her cheeks. The father's face is pale and drawn, his eyes red and swollen, staring blankly ahead, almost unseeing. His arm is around his wife's shoulder, holding her close, but his own body seems to be sagging under an invisible weight.]

[Around them, other mourners—extended family members, friends, and a few classmates of Bianca's—stand in small clusters. Some are openly weeping, their shoulders shaking with quiet sobs. Others stare ahead, their expressions solemn but distant. A few dab at their eyes with handkerchiefs, but their faces suggest they are crying for more than just Bianca. They remember other funerals, other losses, and the grief is layered, complex.]

[A soft, melancholic tune begins to play, perhaps from a small string quartet positioned discreetly to the side, adding a mournful undertone to the scene. The music is slow, each note lingering in the cold air, amplifying the sense of sorrow and finality.]

[The priest raises their hand, and the music fades slightly. With a slow, deliberate gesture, they signal for the casket to be lowered. The parents stiffen, gripping each other tighter. Two attendants step forward, adjusting the straps and mechanisms holding the casket. The crowd seems to collectively hold its breath, waiting for the inevitable.]

[As the casket begins to descend slowly into the ground,

there is a palpable shift in the atmosphere. The soft whirring of the mechanism is the only sound, underscored by the distant cawing of a crow. Bianca's mother lets out a quiet, choked sob, burying her face in her husband's shoulder. The father's eyes are fixed on the casket, his jaw clenched, his body trembling ever so slightly.]

[Some mourners begin to cry more openly, their sobs blending together in a subdued chorus of grief. An elderly relative wipes away tears, looking upward as if searching for some unseen comfort. A young child, too young to fully understand, clutches at their parent's hand, their face a mix of confusion and unease.]

[As the casket lowers further, disappearing inch by inch into the ground, the mourners begin to place flowers and small tokens on the grave. Some throw single roses or lilies, while others drop dirt or earth, each action a symbolic goodbye. The thuds of the earth hitting the casket are muffled but resonant, each one echoing like a quiet drumbeat of finality.]

[Bianca's mother, barely able to stand, reaches out a trembling hand to drop a white rose into the grave. Her hand hovers for a moment, as if unwilling to let go, but then she releases it, the flower falling slowly onto the casket below. She collapses against her husband, her body wracked with sobs. The father, though struggling to hold back his own tears, remains stoic, his eyes still fixed on the grave, his lips moving in silent prayer or perhaps a final, unheard goodbye.]

[The other mourners continue to add their flowers and tokens, each one a small gesture of remembrance, yet also a reminder of their own past losses. Some share quiet words with each other, brief exchanges of comfort and shared pain. Others stand in silence, their eyes distant, caught in their own memories.]

[As the casket reaches the bottom of the grave, the priest steps forward again, speaking softly, but again, the words are indistinct. The crowd bows their heads, and there is a moment of collective stillness—a final, shared breath before the end. The priest gestures toward the sky, then toward the ground, as if to signify the passage of the soul from earth to whatever lies beyond.]

[A moment of silence follows, only broken by the quiet weeping of Bianca's mother and the occasional sniffle or sigh from the mourners. The scene holds this solemn stillness for a few moments longer, letting the weight of the loss settle in.]

[Gradually, the crowd begins to disperse. Some linger, placing a hand on the shoulders of Bianca's parents, offering a few quiet words of condolence. Others turn and walk away slowly, their heads bowed, their expressions weary. The parents remain by the grave, holding each other, staring down into the ground where their daughter now rests. Their tears continue to flow, but their faces remain mostly blank, as if numb from the enormity of the grief.]

[The music resumes, a soft, mournful melody that drifts through the cemetery as the scene fades. The tree's branches sway gently in the breeze, the leaves rustling like a quiet, sorrowful whisper. The light dims slowly, leaving the parents alone by the grave, the final two figures standing in the dim twilight of loss.]

[The stage darkens completely, marking the end of the scene.]

[End Scene 4]

III

Act 3: Life Goes On

Scene 1: School

[The stage is set to represent various locations within a high school: a classroom with rows of desks, a hallway lined with lockers, and a small common area or cafeteria with tables and chairs. The lighting is bright and natural, giving the scene a sense of an ordinary school day. The background noise is filled with the typical sounds of a bustling school—students chatting, lockers opening and closing, the occasional bell ringing to signal the change of classes.]

[The scene opens in the classroom. The desks are arranged in neat rows, each occupied by a student. The teacher stands at the front, writing notes on the whiteboard, explaining a lesson with a calm, practiced cadence. The room is filled with the soft murmur of students taking notes, flipping through textbooks, and occasionally whispering to each other. There is a noticeable calm, a routine normalcy.]

[A new student sits at the desk that once belonged to Bianca. They are focused on the lesson, occasionally raising their hand to answer a question or jotting down notes. The desk is unremarkable, just like the others, and there is no indication that it was ever associated with Bianca. The teacher, without missing a beat, continues the lesson, pointing at the board and asking questions to the class. The students respond with varying degrees of enthusiasm, but there is no mention of Bianca or any sign that she was ever a part of this classroom.]

[The bell rings, signaling the end of the period. The students begin to pack their bags, chatting with one another as they stand up and head toward the door. The new student remains at their desk for a moment, organizing their belongings, then gets up and follows the others out. The teacher erases the board and prepares for the next class, their actions methodical and routine.]

[The lights shift, transitioning to the hallway. Students are moving back and forth, some heading to their next class, others standing by their lockers, exchanging notes, or chatting about upcoming events. Bianca's old locker, now emptied and reassigned, is being used by another student. The locker is decorated with a few photos and magnets, indistinguishable from the others surrounding it. There is no trace of Bianca—no memorial, no signs of remembrance. It's just another locker in a long row of lockers.]

[A group of friends stand nearby, discussing plans for the weekend. They are animated, laughing, and talking over each other, their voices filled with excitement and anticipation. One of them opens their locker, grabs a book, and slams it shut, turning to join the conversation. Another student passes by, headphones in, nodding to the beat of the music, completely absorbed in their own world. The conversations overlap, filled with mundane topics like homework, sports, and parties.]

[A teacher walks down the hallway, a stack of papers in hand, greeting students as they pass by. They stop to chat with a small group, offering reminders about an upcoming test. The students nod, half-listening, already distracted by their own conversations. The teacher moves on, heading into a classroom, and the students continue with their discussions, their expressions relaxed and carefree.]

[The lights shift again, transitioning to the common area or cafeteria. Several tables are occupied by groups of students eating lunch, sharing jokes, and discussing the latest school gossip. A few students are standing in line at the cafeteria counter, while others are moving between tables, waving to friends or stopping briefly to chat. The atmosphere is lively and casual, a typical day at school.]

[At one table, a group of students, some of whom were friends with Bianca, are laughing and talking animatedly. One of them tells a funny story about something that happened in class, and the others burst into laughter. There is no mention of Bianca, no lingering sadness or reflection. They have moved on, their lives continuing without much interruption.]

[A student nearby mentions a memorial event that was

held months ago, but it's a passing comment, said without much emotion or significance. The conversation quickly shifts back to more immediate concerns—upcoming exams, weekend plans, the latest rumors circulating around the school. The mention of Bianca is like a brief shadow that passes and then is gone, barely noticed.]

[Two students walk by, engaged in a conversation about an upcoming party. They pause near the table, briefly exchanging a few words with the group, then move on, laughing about something else. The cafeteria remains filled with the hum of activity, the clatter of trays and utensils, the occasional shout or burst of laughter. The atmosphere is light, almost buoyant.]

[The scene lingers for a moment longer, capturing the mundane, unremarkable reality of the school day. The students continue their routines—eating, chatting, moving from one place to another. There is no sign that anything has changed, no visible reminder of Bianca's absence. Life at the school flows on seamlessly, undisturbed.]

[The lights dim slightly, signaling the end of the scene. The sound of the school bell rings once more, blending into the background noise of voices and footsteps, as the stage slowly fades to black.]

[End Scene 1]

Scene 2: Friends and Family

[The stage is divided into several distinct areas to represent various locations—a cozy café, a living room in a student's home, a small park bench, and a quiet corner of Bianca's family home. The lighting is soft and warm for the café and home settings, while the park bench and family home are dimly lit, creating a contrast between the social vibrancy and solitary reflection.]

[The scene opens in the café. A group of students, some of whom were Bianca's friends, sit around a table by the window. Sunlight streams through, casting patterns on the table. They are chatting animatedly, sipping on coffee and eating pastries. The atmosphere is lively, with the ambient sounds of a bustling café—clinking cups, the hiss of the espresso machine, and soft background music.]

[One friend leans forward, laughing at a story another is telling about a mishap in their last class. They are all engaged, focused on the present moment. The conversation flows easily, moving from topic to topic—plans for the upcoming weekend, a recent movie they watched, and a new student who has caught their attention. Their expressions are relaxed, and there is a sense of camaraderie in their body language.]

[As the story reaches its punchline, the group bursts into laughter. One friend wipes a tear of laughter from their eye, nudging another playfully. There is no mention of Bianca; her absence is neither felt nor acknowledged. The group has found new rhythms, new dynamics, and she has become a distant memory, if even that.]

[The lights shift, transitioning smoothly to a student's home. A small group of friends, different from the café group but still connected to Bianca in some way, are sprawled on a living room floor, surrounded by textbooks and notebooks. A couple of them sit on a couch, while one leans against the wall, typing something on a laptop. They are studying together, but their focus is intermittent, often breaking into jokes or side conversations.]

[One friend mentions an upcoming trip they are planning, and the group quickly dives into discussing potential destinations, logistics, and excitement about getting away. They pull out a travel magazine, pointing at pictures, dreaming of the places they'll visit. There is an undercurrent of anticipation and eagerness in their voices, a youthful energy that carries them forward.]

[The focus subtly lingers on an empty chair in the corner for a moment—a brief, silent reminder of Bianca's absence. But it is quickly overshadowed by the lively conversation continuing around it. The group has moved on, and there is no space for lingering grief in this moment of planning and future excitement.]

[The lights shift again, transitioning to a park bench in a small, quiet park. The scene shows a couple sitting on the bench, deep in conversation, their bodies turned slightly towards each other. They are discussing their future, talking softly about college plans, internships, and what lies ahead. They share a few quiet laughs, a comfortable ease between them.]

[A jogger runs past them, a dog on a leash trotting alongside, barking happily. A mother with a stroller crosses in the background, pausing to adjust a blanket around her child. Life moves steadily around them, the scene filled with small, mundane moments that symbolize continuity. The couple remains engaged in their discussion, oblivious to the world around them, absorbed in each other's presence and their own personal journeys.]

[The lights dim slightly, focusing now on Bianca's family home. The space is quiet, almost eerily so. The living room is dimly lit, the curtains half-drawn, casting long shadows across the floor. Bianca's mother sits on the couch, staring blankly at the television. The sound is on, but it is clear she isn't paying attention. She holds a mug in her hands, occasionally bringing it to her lips, but it's more of a reflex than a conscious action.]

[There is a weariness to her posture, her eyes distant as she gazes past the screen. She glances at a small side table where a few framed photographs are placed. One of them is a picture of Bianca, smiling, perhaps from a school event or a family gathering. The mother's eyes linger on the photograph for a moment, her face softening with a fleeting sense of loss. But then she looks away, her expression returning to one of numb acceptance. She takes a sip from her mug and sets it down, reaching for the remote and changing the channel, the flicker of the TV screen lighting her face in different shades.]

[In a nearby room, Bianca's father is sitting at a desk, sorting through paperwork. His expression is focused, determined, as he flips through pages, occasionally marking something with a pen. His movements are deliberate, mechanical, as if he's lost in the task as a way to avoid other thoughts. He pauses for a moment, his eyes drifting to a framed picture of the family on his desk. His face tightens, a brief flicker of pain crosses his features, but he quickly shakes it off, returning to the paperwork with a heavy sigh.]

[The lighting shifts again, transitioning back to the café. The group of friends are getting up from their seats, gathering their belongings, still chatting away. They put on their jackets, some checking their phones, others discussing where to go next. There's a lightness in their steps, a sense of moving forward. One friend suggests going to a new shop nearby, and the group eagerly agrees, heading for the door together.]

[As they exit, the focus moves back to the park bench.

The couple stands up, still talking softly to each other, and begins to walk down the path, their voices blending into the ambient sounds of the park. The jogger circles back, running in the opposite direction now, the dog still trotting happily beside them. A gentle breeze rustles the leaves on the trees, the scene calm and serene.]

[The lights fade out slowly, the stage quieting down, leaving only the soft hum of life continuing, uninterrupted.]

[End Scene 2]

Scene 3: Bianca's Grave

[The stage is set to represent a small, secluded section of a cemetery. The lighting is dim, with a muted gray tone that suggests an overcast sky. The atmosphere is still, almost eerily quiet, with the faint sound of a breeze rustling through the trees in the background. A few old, weathered headstones are scattered across the stage, each one slightly leaning or covered in moss, adding to the sense of neglect.]

[At the center of the stage is Bianca's grave. The headstone is simple, modestly inscribed with her name, dates, and a short epitaph. However, the stone is beginning to weather, with faint cracks and discoloration marring its surface. The surrounding grass is overgrown, and weeds have started to encroach on the edges of the grave. The once neatly maintained plot is now untidy, the earth slightly sunken, a clear sign that time has passed.]

[There are no fresh flowers on the grave, only a few wilted remnants from the funeral, now dry and brittle. A small vase lies on its side, empty and forgotten. The scene is stark, almost desolate, with no signs of recent visitors. The grave feels abandoned, a silent testament to the passage of time and the fading of memory.]

[The focus remains on the grave for a long moment, allowing the audience to absorb the quiet desolation. The wind picks up slightly, causing a few dried leaves to scatter across the ground, some catching on the uneven grass around the grave. The cemetery is empty, devoid of any life or movement, reinforcing the isolation of this final resting place.]

[A single crow lands on the headstone, its black feathers a sharp contrast against the weathered gray stone. It caws once, a harsh, grating sound that echoes in the stillness. The crow pecks at the ground for a moment, then flaps its wings and flies off, leaving the grave as silent and lonely as it was before.]

[As the crow departs, a light rain begins to fall. The drops are soft at first, barely noticeable, but they gradually intensify, creating a soft pattering sound on the ground and the headstones. The rain washes over the grave, darkening the stone and causing small rivulets of water to run down the epitaph, further blurring the already fading inscription.]

[The rain continues for a few moments, gradually cleansing the scene, washing away some of the dust and grime that has accumulated on the headstone. Yet, even as the rain falls, the neglect and decay remain evident, a stark reminder that no amount of rain can restore what has been forgotten.]

[The lighting slowly dims, casting the grave in a deeper shadow. The cemetery becomes darker, more somber, as the day turns to twilight. The rain softens to a drizzle, then stops altogether, leaving the grave glistening with moisture, the only sign of recent change in an otherwise unchanging landscape.]

[A distant sound of church bells tolling faintly in the background is heard, signaling the passage of time and marking the end of another day. The bells are slow and deliberate, each toll resonating in the still air, a melancholic reminder of the relentless march of time.]

[The focus remains on Bianca's grave, now shrouded in shadow and silence. The scene holds for a long, reflective moment, emphasizing the solitude and abandonment. The world has moved on, indifferent to the tragedy that unfolded, leaving behind only a neglected grave as a fading memory of a life once lived.]

[The stage gradually fades to black, leaving the grave and the cemetery in complete darkness. The final sound is the soft rustle of the wind through the trees, a quiet whisper of nature continuing its course, indifferent to the human emotions tied to the place.]

[End Scene 3]

www.ingramcontent.com/pod-product-compliance
Lightning Source LLC
Chambersburg PA
CBHW052231150726
48002CB00003B/1385